KU-161-019

WEST SUSSEX INSTITUTE OF
HIGHER EDUCATION LIBRARY

AUTHOR
MAHY, M

TITLE
BOY WITH TWO
SHADOWS

WS 2036911 5

CLASS No
P/MAH

This reillustrated edition
first published 1987
Text © Margaret Mahy 1971, 1987
Illustrations © Jenny Williams 1987
All rights reserved

Phototypeset in Great Britain
by Gee Graphics Limited, London
Printed in West Germany
for J.M. Dent & Sons Ltd
Aldine House, 33 Welbeck Street, London W1M 8LX

British Library Cataloguing in Publication Data
Mahy, Margaret
    The boy with two shadows. ——— New ed.
    I. Title   II. Williams, Jenny
    823 [J]   PZ7
    ISBN 0-460-06241-7

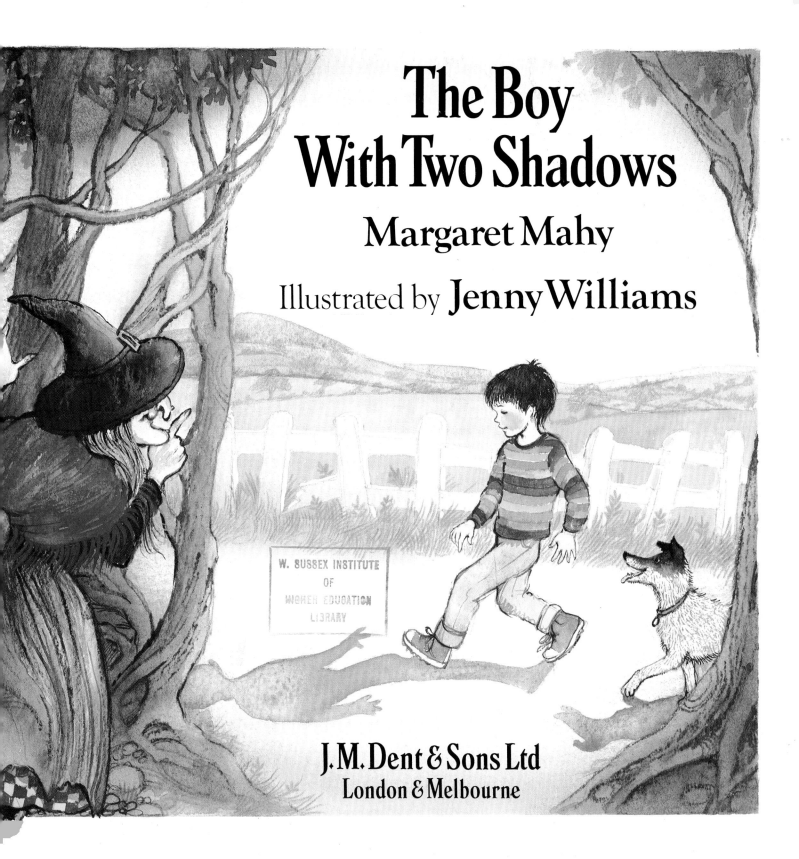

The Boy
With Two Shadows

Margaret Mahy

Illustrated by Jenny Williams

W. SUSSEX INSTITUTE
OF
HIGHER EDUCATION
LIBRARY

J. M. Dent & Sons Ltd
London & Melbourne

There was once a little boy who took great care of his
shadow. He was quite a careful little boy with buttons
and shoes and all the odd pieces. But most especially
he was careful with his shadow because he knew he
had only one, and it had to last him all his life.

He always tried to manage things so
that his shadow didn't trail in the dust.
If he just couldn't keep it out of the dust
he hurried to get to a clean place for it.

The boy took such care of his shadow
that a witch noticed it.
She stopped the boy
on his way home from school.

"I've been watching you," she said.
"I like the way you look after your shadow."

"I don't want to wear it out," said the boy. "It's the only one I've got."

"True! True!" said the witch approvingly. "Always look after your shadow! Now, I want someone reliable to look after *my* shadow while I'm away on holiday. You know what a nuisance a shadow can be when you're trying to have a good time."

"My shadow isn't any trouble," said the boy doubtfully.

"I need a good shadow-sitter," the witch declared. "But I'm not going to leave it with just anybody. I've chosen you to take care of it."

The boy did not like to argue with a witch.

"All right," he said, "but hurry back, won't you?"

The witch bared her teeth in a witch smile, which was quite wicked-looking, though she was trying to be pleasant.

"If you look after my shadow properly," she promised, "you shall have a whole magic spell of your own. I'll choose a good one just for you."

Then she fastened her shadow on to the boy's shadow, climbed on to her broom, and made off – light and free as thistledown, with sunlight all around her and no bobbling black patch chasing at her heels.

The boy now had two shadows. One was his own. The other was the fierce, crooked, thorny shadow of the witch.

The witch's shadow was
the worst-behaved shadow in the world.
Usually, shadows have to copy their people –
but the witch's shadow had ideas
of its own. When the little boy went to buy
apples, the witch's shadow rummaged among the shadows
of the fruit. It put the shadows of all the oranges beside the bananas and
mixed up the shadows of the peaches. Everything was higgledy-piggledy.

The man in the fruit shop said, "Bananas with
the shadows of oranges! Oranges with no shadows at all!
People will think I'm cheating them. Throw that shadow out!"
The little boy didn't like to turn the witch's shadow
loose on its own. He rushed out of the shop without
his apples.

At home, during tea, the witch's shadow stretched itself long and leaped all over the wall. It took the shadow from the clock, and the clock stopped. Then it terrified the parrot into fits, and pulled the shadow-tail of the dog's shadow.

"Really!" said the little boy's mother. "That wicked shadow is making me spill my tea and cut the cake crooked. Couldn't you keep it outside?"

The boy didn't want
his mother to spill her tea,
but he was determined to
look after the witch's shadow.
From then on he had his tea in the kitchen on his own.

He became so clever at keeping the witch's shadow from getting into mischief and wickedness that at last it couldn't find anything wicked to do.

Naturally this made it very cross.

Suddenly it thought of something very, very mean – so mean that you would think even a witch's shadow would be ashamed. It started teasing and terrifying the little boy's *own* shadow. It was terrible to see. The boy's shadow had always been treated kindly. It did not know what to do now about this new, fierce thing that pushed it out of gardens and gutters, that pinched it, prodded it, poked it – treading on its heels as they hurried down the road.

One day the boy's shadow could bear this no longer. In broad daylight the boy, going home to lunch, saw his two shadows – short and squat – running beside him. The witch's shadow nipped his own shadow with her long witch fingernails. It gave a great bound and broke free from his feet. Away, away it flew on its own, leaping silently, tumbling off like a bit of wastepaper blown by a secret wind.

Then it was gone. The little boy ran after it, but it was nowhere to be seen. He stood still. He listened. The warm summer afternoon was so quiet he could hear the witch shadow laughing – or rather, he heard the echo of laughing (because, as you know, an echo is the shadow of sound, and sometimes the sound of a shadow).

So there was the little boy with only one shadow again –
but it was the *wrong* shadow. His real shadow was quite gone,
and now he had only the witch's left.

It was more like having a thorn bush at his heels than a
proper shadow – a thorn bush that could pull faces, too.
People stared and pointed, and shrank away. As for the
boy, he felt sad and lonely without his own shadow. He
tried to enjoy having the witch's shadow, but it was like
trying to pet a wild wolf or thistle.

At last the witch came back. She wrote the boy a letter in grey ink on black paper, telling him to meet her that night at midnight and to be sure to bring her shadow with him.

(Thank goodness it was a bright moonlit night
or it might have been extremely difficult
to find that wretched shadow, which sometimes
hid away from him.)

"Aha!" said the witch when she saw it,
and she whisked it back in half-a-minute
less than no time – or even faster.

"And here's your spell," she said. "Defrost it, bake it, and then eat it."
The spell was written on a quick-frozen sausage-roll.

"What will it do?" asked the boy.
"Turn you into a camel," said the witch. "A white racing camel – or a
Bactrian, or any sort of camel you like – but just for an hour or two."

The little boy didn't really want to turn himself into a camel – even for an hour or two. He wanted his own shadow back again.

"Your fierce shadow has chased mine away," he told the witch sternly.

The witch sniggered a bit in a witch-like fashion.

"Well, my dear," she said, "you can't expect everything to be easy, you know. Anyhow, I feel I've paid you handsomely for your trouble. Run off home now."

And off she went, taking her shadow with her. It didn't even bother to wave goodbye.

The boy went home shadowless through a moonlit world of shadows. Trees had shadows. Fence posts had shadows. Sleeping cows had sleeping shadows around them. The boy felt very lonely.

But as he walked home, something dark and mysterious came to meet him. It copied everything he did. He took a step and *it* took a step. He waved, and it waved back. Softly and shyly, as if it were ashamed of itself, his own shadow sidled towards him. It had been hiding among other shadows, keeping an eye on him. Now it slipped along toe-to-toe with him just as it had always done.

The little boy thought for a moment. The wicked witch-shadow was gone. He could turn into any sort of camel he liked – and a mischievous camel could have a lot of fun at the school fancy-dress ball – just for an hour or two. Best of all, he had his own shadow back again.

He was so pleased he did a strange little dance in the moonlight while, toe-to-toe, his shadow danced beside him.